Karen's Kittycat Club

**Here are some other books
about Karen
that you might enjoy:**

Karen's Witch

Karen's Roller Skates

Karen's Worst Day

Karen's School Picture

Little Sister

Karen's Kittycat Club

Ann M. Martin

Illustrations by Susan Tang

A
LITTLE APPLE
PAPERBACK

SCHOLASTIC INC.
New York Toronto London Auckland Sydney

ISBN 0-590-44264-3

31 30 29 28 27 26 25 24   8 9/9 0/0

Printed in the U.S.A.   40

First Scholastic printing, June 1989

For Jennifer Esty—
a big sister

Karen Two-Two

This year, in second grade, my teacher read a very funny book to our class. I liked it a lot. The book was called *Jacob Two-Two Meets the Hooded Fang*.

My name is Karen Brewer. But sometimes I think it should be Karen Two-Two. Why? Because of all the twos in my life. The biggest two is my two families. That's right. I have *two* families. So does Andrew. He's my brother. I am six and Andrew is four.

Andrew and I have two families because of our parents. A long time ago, our daddy was married to our mommy. Then they got divorced. Daddy married a woman named Elizabeth. She's our stepmother. After that, Mommy married a man named Seth. Mostly, Andrew and I live with Mommy and Seth. But every other weekend, we live with Daddy and Elizabeth. Two houses, two families.

Mommy and Seth's house is little. The only people who live there are Mommy, Seth, Andrew, and me. Oh, and Rocky and Midgie. But they're not people. Rocky is a cat and Midgie is a dog.

Daddy and Elizabeth's house is big. It's gigundo. Which is a good thing, because a lot of people live in the big house: Daddy, Elizabeth, Andrew, me, Charlie, Sam, David Michael, and Kristy. Oh, and Boo-Boo and Shannon. Boo-Boo is Daddy's fat, mean cat. Shannon is David Michael's puppy. She is sweet and fluffy and playful. I love Shannon. But Shannon loves David Michael more than me. That's because she sees David Michael more than me.

Charlie, Sam, David Michael, and Kristy are Elizabeth's kids. They are my stepbrothers and stepsister. Sam and Charlie are really old. They go to high school. David Michael is seven, just a little older than me. Kristy is thirteen.

So, two houses, one big and one little. Two families, one big and one little. And two of lots of other things. Since Andrew and I go back and forth between our houses so often, we each have two pairs of sneakers,

two pairs of jeans, two bicycles (well, Andrew has two tricycles), two teddy bears, and more. I have two stuffed cats, Moosie and Goosie, and two pieces of Tickly, my special blanket. We keep one of each thing at the little house, and one at the big house. That way, we don't have to pack a lot of stuff when we go to Daddy's or Mommy's.

Karen Two-Two. Andrew Two-Two.

But there is one thing I do *not* have two of — and I wish I *did*. That is my stepsister. Kristy is really great. I wish I had another sister just like her at the little house. Kristy is my friend. She plays with me. She reads to me. She talks to me. I love Kristy so, so much.

Kristy also takes care of me. She is a baby-sitter. She and her friends have a club called the Baby-sitters Club. It is very cool. The girls meet three times a week, and they get baby-sitting jobs. They earn lots of money. Sometimes the girls in the club have sleepovers. Or parties. I wish I could be in a club like Kristy's. But how do you start a club?

Anyway, I'm not old enough to baby-sit. Yet. Someday I will be. Then I will join the Baby-sitters Club.

I looked out my bedroom window. I was at the little house. Andrew and I were waiting for Mommy to drive us to the big house. We were going to spend the weekend with Daddy and Elizabeth and Kristy and all our brothers.

We could not wait. Weekends at the big house are fun. Something exciting usually happens. Once my friend Hannie and I had a scary adventure. Once I broke my wrist. Sometimes Daddy takes everybody for a drive, or we go to an amusement park.

"Karen!" Mommy called. "Andrew! Time to go! Get your knapsacks!"

"Hurray!" I shouted.

"Hurray!" shouted Andrew from his room.

We clattered down the stairs.

We were on our way to the big house!

Cats and Dogs

Saturday morning is the best, best time of any weekend at Daddy's. That's what I think. I wake up in my room at the big house, and the day stretches ahead of me. And I know I'll go back to sleep that night in my room at the big house.

I try to make Saturdays as nice as I can. That Saturday, the day after Andrew and I went to Daddy's, I put on my lucky rabbit's foot. I fastened it to my belt loop. My rabbit's foot is orange and fuzzy. But it is not as fuzzy as it used to be. That's because I pat it so much the fur is coming off.

Maybe I should have been wearing my rabbit's foot the day I fell roller-skating. If I had been wearing it, I might not have broken my wrist. But I did break it. I had to go to the hospital and get a cast and everything. It was exciting. Well, it was exciting at first. After awhile, the cast was boring. I could not go roller-skating or ride my bike or anything. But guess what? The cast is gone! Dr. Humphrey took it off two weeks ago. My wrist is all better.

After I put on my rabbit's foot, I put a lucky stone in my pocket. Then I tied my favorite purple ribbon in my hair. I was ready for Saturday.

"Good morning! Good morning, every-one!" I called as I ran downstairs.

"Good morning, Karen," five voices answered.

I found Daddy, Elizabeth, David Michael, Andrew, and Kristy in the kitchen, just beginning their breakfasts. Shannon and

Boo-Boo were eating, too. Shannon was eating on the floor near the dishwasher. Elizabeth had spread about three thousand newspapers under her dishes. Shannon makes a gigundo mess when she eats.

Guess where Boo-Boo was eating? Up on the counter. My friend Hannie thinks that's gross, but we have to let Boo-Boo eat there. Shannon is just a puppy. So she's a big tease. Sometimes she pesters Boo-Boo while he's trying to eat.

In case you're wondering, Shannon is a Bernese mountain dog. She's black and white and fluffy. She'll grow up to be a pretty big dog. Boo-Boo is a gray tiger cat. He's old and fat and mean. I hardly ever play with Boo-Boo. He doesn't play much anyway. Mostly he sleeps or scratches people.

Rocky, Seth's cat, is much nicer than Boo-Boo. For one thing, he is young. I think he is only about a year old. Maybe a little more. And he is polite. He does not scratch people.

He does not scratch other cats. Rocky is pretty, too. His fur is orange-y, and he licks it a lot to keep it sleek and clean. Midgie, Seth's dog, is a mutt. But that's okay. He's a nice little dog, even if we don't know what kind he is. Andrew loves Midgie. Sometimes, when we're at the little house, Midgie sleeps on Andrew's bed.

Boy, are Andrew and I lucky to be two-twos. This way, we have four pets.

I thought about that after I had finished my breakfast. I went outside and sat on our front steps.

Nancy Dawes is my best friend at the little house. She lives next door to us. She does not have any pets at all.

Hannie Papadakis is my best friend here at the big house. Hannie and her brother and sister have two pets. They have a poodle named Noodle and a turtle named Myrtle. Myrtle is not much fun, but Noodle is.

Amanda Delaney is a friend who lives sort of across the street from the big house.

She and her brother have one pet, a cat named Priscilla.

"Karen! Karen!" a voice called just then.

It came from across the street. It was Hannie Papadakis, my big-house best friend. She sounded very excited.

Pat the Cat

"What is it?" I shouted.

I stood up. I saw Hannie running across our lawn.

"Guess what? Guess what?" she called.

I began jumping up and down. That was how excited Hannie was making me. "I can't guess. Tell me," I cried. "Tell me quick!"

Hannie slowed to a stop. She could hardly catch her breath. "We," she began, and then she had to start over. "We — we got a kitten!"

"A kitten?! Oh, Hannie. You are so lucky!"

"Linny and I have always wanted a cat," said Hannie. Linny is Hannie's older brother. He's eight. He and David Michael are friends. Hannie is seven. We're in the same class at school. (I skipped first grade.) Sari, Hannie's little sister, is just two.

"What did you name him?" I asked.

"Her," Hannie corrected me. "She's a her. And her name is Pat."

"Oh!" I exclaimed. "So when she's all grown up she'll be Pat the cat."

"Right," replied Hannie. "Pat the cat, Noodle the poodle, and Myrtle the turtle."

"Three pets," I said.

Hannie nodded proudly.

I could not help thinking again about how lucky Andrew and I are to be two-twos and have more pets than any of my friends. Maybe that wasn't a nice thing to think, but I thought it anyway.

"Karen, come over and meet Pat," said Hannie.

"Okay," I replied. I stuck my head in our

front door. I told Daddy and Elizabeth where I was going. Then Hannie and I ran to her house.

"Pat is on the sun porch," Hannie told me. "We put all her stuff there. We put her toys and food and litter box on the floor. We spread out an old sweater for her to sleep on. I think she feels safe on the porch. She's too little to go roaming around the house." (Hannie's house is as big as Daddy's.)

Hannie and I tiptoed through the door to the porch.

"She might be asleep," Hannie whispered.

We checked the sweater. No Pat.

"Sometimes she hides," said Hannie.

We peered under the chairs and tables. No Pat.

Then something furry brushed against my ankle. I looked down. There was a fuzzy black kitten. She was carrying a toy in her mouth.

"Aw, Hannie," I exclaimed. "Look at her! She's so cute."

Hannie grinned. She and I tossed Pat's toy around for her. While we were playing, I thought of something.

"Hey, Hannie," I said. "It's neat that you have a cat."

"I know. Pat is our very first one."

"But there's something even better. Now you and Amanda and I all have cats," I pointed out to her. "We have Pat, Priscilla, and Boo-Boo. And Rocky at the little house."

"Yeah," said Hannie. She didn't sound too interested. I guessed that was because she doesn't like Amanda very much.

But *I* was interested. Hannie and Amanda and I live right near each other. And now we all have cats.

"Look!" said Hannie. "Look what Pat can do."

Hannie held up a piece of string. She dangled it above Pat. Pat leaped up on her hind legs. She batted at the string.

I began to giggle. "Pat's dancing!" I cried.

Hannie laughed, too.

We let Pat dance until she got tired. Then she lay down on the sweater and fell asleep. Just like that.

"She's so cute," I said to Hannie. I think I had already said that about three thousand times.

"Yeah," agreed Hannie softly.

16

"I better go," I told her. "It's lunchtime. I'll see you later."

"Okay," replied Hannie. "See you!"

I left Hannie's house.

I was getting an idea.

The Kittycat Club

This was my idea. Hannie and Amanda and I all had cats. That meant we had something in common. And since we had something in common, we could start a club. We could start a cat club.

Let me see. What could we call it? The Cat Club? The Cat-Lovers Club? The We ♡ Cats Club? The . . . the Kittycat Club! That was it! It sounded great. The name was perfect. No, it was purrfect. (Get it?)

I was so excited that I began to run. I ran

to our front steps and flopped down on them. I thought for awhile.

The Kittycat Club.

What would we do at our club meetings? I mean, what would be the reason for having the club?

Three people, three cats . . . Hmm.

Maybe we could learn about cats. We could learn where they came from and how their insides work and how they meow and

purr. But no. The more I thought about that, the more boring it sounded. We'd probably just have to look up a lot of stuff at the library. I wanted our club to be more fun. And I wanted our cats to come to the club meetings. Cats would not be allowed in the library.

Maybe we could teach our cats tricks. Priscilla knows how to shake. And Pat is young. She could learn lots of tricks. But not Boo-Boo, I thought sadly. Boo-Boo is too old and fat and grumpy to learn tricks.

I was sitting on the steps with my chin in my hands. I had run out of ideas.

"Hey, there!" said Kristy. She came out of the house and sat down next to me. "What are you doing?"

"I'm thinking about the Kittycat Club," I told her. "Hannie got a kitten. Now she and Amanda and I all have cats. I think we should start a cat club. The Kittycat Club."

"But Hannie and Amanda don't like each other," Kristy pointed out.

"I know. Maybe they could learn to like

20

each other if we were in a club, though. I think it would work. I really do. I just don't know what our club would be for. And I don't know how to start it. Tell me about the Baby-sitters Club. Please, Kristy. *Please?* How did you start it?"

Kristy sighed. "Okay," she said. "But it's a long story. Let's go inside. We'll get our lunches and take them in the backyard. We'll have a picnic. And I'll tell you how I started the Baby-sitters Club."

Kristy's Club

Kristy and I went into the kitchen. Another good thing about Saturdays is lunchtime. We have several names for Saturday lunch. One is "Smorgasbord." One is "Every Man for Himself." One is "Fantasy Food." What it means is that we put practically all the food in the house out on the kitchen table. We put out bread and mustard and mayonnaise and cheese and cold cuts and pickles and olives and peanut butter and jelly and fruit and salad and potato chips and pretzels and carrot sticks and celery sticks and juice and milk. We can eat whatever we want.

Each week, Sam makes a Dagwood. A Dagwood is a gigundo sandwich. In between the slices of bread he piles ham, bologna, cheese, pickles, potato chips, and lettuce. Sometimes he adds gross stuff like leftover meat loaf. Once he put in three olives.

I always have the exact same lunch: an apple, a celery stick with peanut butter spread in it, some potato chips, and milk. That is a very wonderful meal.

I put my lunch together and waited for Kristy. She was making a peanut butter and banana sandwich. She said that I would not throw up if I took a bite of it. I didn't believe her.

At last we were ready. Kristy and I carried our lunches outside. We did not spill one thing.

"Here's a good spot," said Kristy.

We sat on the ground in front of an oak tree. We balanced our plates in our laps.

"Now tell me about the Baby-sitters Club," I said. Then I remembered to add, "Please."

Kristy smiled. "I thought you were going to say, 'Now tell me a story.'"

"No, tell me about your club."

"All right," said Kristy. "Well, it's really a business. I started it when I saw how hard it sometimes was for Mom to find a sitter for David Michael. She would have to phone lots of people, looking for someone who was free to baby-sit. So I thought it would be great if a mom or a dad could make *one* phone call and reach several baby-sitters at the same time. One of the sitters would probably be free."

I nodded.

"So I got together with some of my friends. We decided we would meet three times a week. Then when parents needed sitters, they could call us during our meetings."

"How did they know when you would be meeting?" I wondered. (I was getting another idea. I needed some important information.)

"We advertised," said Kristy. "We made up fliers."

"Fliers?"

"You know, little posters. We took a piece of paper and wrote down all the information about our club. Things like when we meet, how old we are, what we do, the number to call to reach us. Then we made lots of copies of the paper. We left the fliers in people's mailboxes. We also put an ad in the newspaper.

"People really paid attention to the fliers," Kristy went on. "Right away, they started calling us. We got lots of jobs."

"You *did?*" I said excitedly.

"Yup. Now we're very busy. So we run our club in an official way."

"What do you mean?"

"We elected a president — that's me —a vice-president, a secretary, and a treasurer. Everyone has a job. We think it's the best way to run the club."

"Hmm. A president and stuff. That's

neat," I said. I bit into my celery. It crunched nicely. KER-RUNCH!

Kristy bit into her apple. It crunched, too. KER-RUNCH!

We smiled at each other.

I could not wait to get to my room. I had big plans.

Bring Your Cat!!!

Kristy and I finished our lunches. We carried our plates back to the kitchen. Then I ran to my bedroom.

"Moosie," I said to my stuffed cat, "are we ever going to be busy! We need to make two invitations. And they have to be really good."

In my room are a table and four chairs. They are just the right size for me and Andrew and David Michael. Everyone else in the house is too big for them. Even Kristy.

I put Moosie in one chair. I found my

crayons and some plain paper. Then I sat down next to Moosie.

"Now," I said, "we are going to make two invitations. One for Hannie, one for Amanda. We're going to invite them to join the Kittycat Club. Kristy didn't say anything about invitations, but I'm going to make them anyway. I think invitations would be nice. Don't you, Moosie?"

I pretended that Moosie said yes.

"Okay. Let me think."

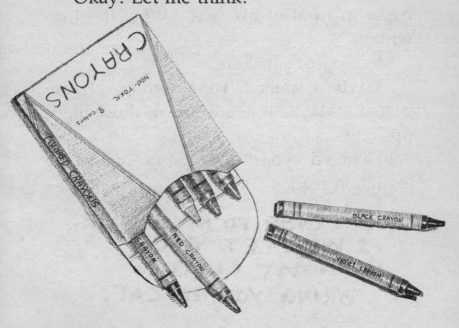

I thought. Then I chose a green crayon. I wrote:

**COME OVER TO MY HOUSE.
I WILL LET YOU JOYN MY CLUB.
BRING YOUR CAT.**

I read it over. It did not sound quite right. Also, I think I had spelled a word wrong. But I wasn't sure.

"Look at this, Moosie," I said. I held the paper in front of his face. "What did I do wrong?"

Moosie just sat there.

"Maybe I spelled 'your' wrong," I suggested. "Maybe it needs one of those high-up commas."

I changed "your" to "you're." Now the invitation read:

**COME OVER TO MY HOUSE.
I WILL LET YOU
JOYN MY CLUB.
BRING YOU'RE CAT.**

30

"I don't know, Moosie. This still isn't right. It isn't like the birthday party invitations that come in the mail. They always start off with 'Join the fun!' Then they say 'Come to a birthday party,' and they say where the party will be, and when."

I thought for awhile. I chose a yellow crayon and a new piece of paper. I wrote

COME JOYN
THE KITTYCAT CLUB!

I had just finished writing CLUB when I realized something. I could not read what I had written. Yellow hardly shows up on white at all.

I started over with red.

COME JOYN
THE KITTYCAT CLUB!

Then I wrote:

WHEN: TODAY.
TIME: THREE : 00.
WHERE: MY HOUSE.

"Hmm. Do you think Hannie and Amanda will know that 'my house' means 'Karen Brewer's house,' Moosie?" I stared at what I had written. "And that time looks funny. How do you write 'three o'clock'?"

I did not want to do it, but I had to ask a grown-up for help. I asked Daddy. He showed me how to fix my mistakes. Then I started over *again*. When I finished Hannie's invitation, it looked like this:

COME JOIN THE KITTYCAT CLUB!
WHEN: TODAY
TIME: 3:00
WHERE: KAREN'S HOUSE
BRING YOUR CAT!!!

"Who would have thought you spell 'join' with an 'i'?" I asked Moosie. "You spell 'joy' with a 'y,' and 'join' sounds like 'joy' with an 'n.' Oh, well."

I had written Hannie's invitation with the

red crayon. I wrote Amanda's with a purple crayon.

"There. All done," I said.

Very carefully, I folded each invitation in half, and then in half again. I put them in envelopes. I wrote Hannie's name on one, and Amanda's name on the other. Then I dashed across the street to Hannie's house. I left her envelope on her front porch. I rang the bell and ran away. I did the same thing with Amanda's envelope at the Delaneys'.

My invitations had been delivered.

Cats, Cats, Cats

At fifteen minutes to three that afternoon, I went looking for Boo-Boo. He had to come to the first meeting of the Kittycat Club. (He would have to come to all of the meetings.)

I wished I had a nice cat like Pat. Or a beautiful cat like Priscilla. But I didn't. I had Boo-Boo. I had scratchy, old, fat Boo-Boo. The good thing about Boo-Boo was that he *is* a cat. Without him, I could not be in my own Kittycat Club.

"Boo-Boo! Boo-Boo!" I called. Where was he?

I looked in the living room. Sometimes he and Shannon curl up together on one of the couches. But the couches were empty.

I looked in the backyard. The backyard was empty.

I looked on the kitchen counter, by Boo-Boo's food dish. The counter was empty.

At last I found Boo-Boo asleep in the laundry basket.

"Come on, you old fat thing," I said.

"HSSS," went Boo-Boo. But I lugged him upstairs anyway.

Boo-Boo did not want to stay in my room, so I had to close the door.

Soon I heard *knock, knock, knock*.

"Who is it?" I called.

"It's Hannie and Pat!"

"Come on in to the Kittycat Club!" I replied.

Hannie opened the door. She put Pat on the floor. Next to Boo-Boo, Pat looked like a flea and Boo-Boo looked like an elephant.

Even so, Pat walked right up to Boo-Boo. She swiped at his paw.

"HSSS," went Boo-Boo again. And *he* swiped at *Pat*.

"Poor Pat!" cried Hannie. She scooped her kitten up.

Suddenly I could hear someone saying, "Nice Priscilla, nice Priscilla."

"Amanda's here," I announced.

"Hooray," said Hannie. (She did not mean it.)

Amanda came into my room. She was holding Priscilla in her arms. Priscilla is a beautiful cat. She's a Persian. Her fur is very long. And it's snowy white. Amanda is nice, but sometimes she talks about Priscilla too much. She's forever saying that Priscilla cost four hundred dollars. That's one reason Hannie doesn't like her.

"Hi," said Amanda. She and Priscilla were standing in the doorway. "I guess this is the Kittycat Club."

"That's right," I said. I made a dive for Boo-Boo. Hannie had put Pat on the bed. Boo-Boo was after the kitten.

36

"Come on in," I told Amanda.

Amanda stepped inside. Pat leaped off the bed. Boo-Boo tore after her.

"Amanda! Amanda! Close the door!" I cried. "They're going to escape!"

Amanda closed it. Just in time.

"Sit down," I said to my friends. They sat on the floor. "Now this is my idea. The Kittycat Club will be a cat-sitting service, just like Kristy's baby-sitting — "

"Hey!" shrieked Amanda. "Hannie Papadakis! Make your kitten stop that! She's going to bother Priscilla."

Too late. Pat pounced on Priscilla's tail. Priscilla jumped a mile. She jumped right over Boo-Boo. Then she turned around and gave Boo-Boo a swat in the face.

Hannie grabbed Pat and hugged her. "Naughty Priscilla," she said.

Amanda grabbed Priscilla and hugged her. "Naughty Pat," she said.

I let Boo-Boo run under the bed.

"Okay, you guys," I said.

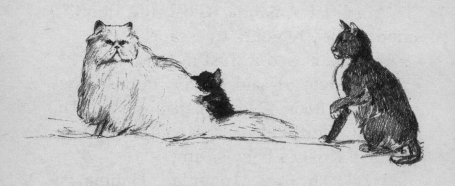

But Hannie and Amanda were walking
toward the door. Their cats were in their
arms.

"Good-bye!" shouted Amanda.

"Wait!" I cried. "Don't you want to make
a lot of money?"

Karen's Cat-sitting
Service

"Make a lot of money?" repeated Amanda.

"Yes," I replied.

"If you earned enough, Amanda, you could buy another four-hundred-dollar cat," said Hannie.

Amanda stuck her tongue out at Hannie. Hannie stuck hers out at Amanda. They glared at each other.

"Come on, you guys," I said. "The Kittycat Club is supposed to be fun. Why don't you put the cats down. Then I'll tell you my idea."

"Well . . . all right," agreed Hannie.

Boo-Boo was still under the bed, so Hannie put Pat on top of the bed. Amanda sat down and put Priscilla in her lap.

The cats were quiet.

"Okay," I said. "See, Kristy has a baby-sitting service." I told my friends about the Baby-sitters Club and how it works.

"But what about the Kittycat Club?" asked Amanda.

"Well, I thought we could do the same thing, except with cats," I replied. "When someone goes away for a few days, we'll take care of their cat. We will stop in at their house to feed the cat and change the litter box. We all have cats so we know how to take care of them."

"Oh!" said Hannie. "Good idea! This sounds like fun. What do we do at our club meetings?"

"We wait for people to call and say that they need us," I answered.

"How do they know we're here?" Amanda wondered. "And how will they know *when* we're here?"

"Good questions," I said. "We advertise. It's the only thing to do."

"Advertise? Like on TV?" asked Hannie. "Commercials?"

"Oh, no," I said. "We just make fliers. Then we put them in people's mailboxes. The fliers will say what we can do, how old we are, and when our meetings are. I'm sure people will start calling us right away. They must need cat-sitters all the time."

"So we just have to make some fliers," said Amanda.

"And we will be rich!" I exclaimed.

"Yeah . . . " said Hannie and Amanda. I could tell they were excited.

But Amanda began to look confused. "How come," she said slowly, "we have to bring our cats to the meetings?"

How come? Hmm. I wasn't sure. It just seemed like the thing to do if you belonged to the Kittycat Club.

"Because . . . because this is the Kittycat Club, that's why," I replied. I felt a little embarrassed. "Listen. Before the cats start fighting again, why don't you take Pat and Priscilla home. Come back tomorrow for our second meeting. We will make the fliers then. Okay?"

"Okay," agreed my friends.

"This meeting," I said, "is over." (I said that to make the meeting official.)

"How is the Kittycat Club?" Kristy asked me that evening.

It was bedtime. She had already read me a story and tucked me in.

I grinned. "It's great! Amanda and Hannie came over this afternoon. They brought their cats. The Kittycat Club is going to cat-sit. Just like your club baby-sits. Tomorrow we'll have another meeting. We'll make fliers."

"Like the fliers I told you about?"

"Just like them."

"Karen," Kristy began, "not every club works. Not every business is a success."

"But the Kittycat Club will be," I told her. "I just know it . . . Moosie knows it, too. Here, Moosie. Kiss Kristy good night."

I made Moosie kiss my big sister. Then Kristy kissed Moosie and me. "Good night," she said. "And good luck with the Kittycat Club."

We Are Cat-Sitters!

"Excuse me! Excuse me!" I called.

It was the second meeting of the Kittycat Club. No one was paying any attention to me. Pat and Priscilla and Boo-Boo were chasing each other. Hannie and Amanda were arguing. I tried to think what my teacher would do if no one in our class was paying attention. Then I remembered.

I clapped my hands loudly.

The cats jumped.

Amanda and Hannie glared at me.

"We are *trying* to have a meeting," I said. "Now the first thing we have to do is make the fliers."

"What goes on a flier?" asked Amanda.

"Our names and ages," said Hannie.

"How much we charge," I added.

"How much is that?" Amanda wanted to know.

My friends and I looked at each other.

"A dollar a day?" suggested Hannie.

"That doesn't sound like much money," replied Amanda.

"How about three dollars a day? Then we can divide it up between us," I said. "We'd each get a whole dollar."

"Okay," said Hannie.

"We have to put our meeting times on the fliers," Amanda reminded us. "When will we meet?"

"I guess on the weekends when I'm here visiting Daddy," I replied. "Hannie, I see you in school, but not you, Amanda." (Hannie and I go to one school, Amanda goes to a different school.) "So our meetings will be every other Saturday. How about from two o'clock until three o'clock?"

"Okay," said Amanda and Hannie.

"What if someone needs to call for a cat-sitter, but not on one of those Saturdays?" asked Hannie.

"Hmm," I said slowly. "I guess we ought to say to call one of us at home."

"Which one of us?" said Amanda right away.

Hannie looked thoughtful. "Maybe me. Most of the jobs are going to be around here. Right in this neighborhood. Well, Karen wouldn't be here, and Amanda isn't at home as much as I am."

This sounded good. We wrote down all the information on a piece of paper. The paper looked very full. It also looked nice. The first line said:

WE ARE CAT-SITTERS! WE LOVE CATS!

Hannie and Amanda and I spent a long time making fliers. We made one after another. When we thought we had made a million of them, we counted. We had made twelve. So we made some more.

Finally, the fliers were finished. Priscilla and Boo-Boo were hissing at each other. Pat was batting Boo-Boo's tail around.

"I think we should go home," said Hannie.

"You can't!" I cried. "We have to choose a president and a vice-president and a secretary. It's too bad we don't have one more person in the Kittycat Club. Then we could choose a treasurer, too."

"Oh, well," said Amanda.

"How do we choose the president?" asked Hannie.

"Easy," I said. "I think I should be the president. The Kittycat Club was my idea. But we could vote, if you want."

"Vote!" cried Hannie and Amanda.

So we voted. Amanda voted for herself,

Hannie voted for herself, and I voted for myself.

The same thing happened when we voted for the vice-president and the secretary.

"Now what?" asked Hannie.

"How about drawing our names out of a . . . " (Amanda looked around my room.) " . . . a box. See that shoe box? We'll use that. We'll take three pieces of paper. We'll each write our name on one piece. Then we'll fold the papers and put them in the box. The first paper we pull out will be the name of our president. The second one will be our vice-president. The one that's left will be our secretary. Okay?"

"Okay!" said Hannie, grinning.

But I was not so happy. I deserved to be the president of the Kittycat Club. No one else should have a chance. But no one else agreed with me.

So we put our names in the shoe box. My friends let me choose the first piece of paper. I opened it up. The name on it was Amanda. Amanda smiled.

Hannie drew next, and she drew my name for the vice-president.

"I guess that means I'm the secretary," said Hannie.

"And I'm the president!" cried Amanda. "All *right*!" She was grinning so wide, her mouth looked like it might slide off her face.

"But I," I said crossly, "am only the vice-president."

"That's better than being the secretary," Hannie pointed out.

"I should be the president," I said. "The Kittycat Club was my idea."

"But we didn't vote for you for president," said Amanda.

"Yeah, you voted for yourselves."

Amanda shrugged. "I'll only be in the Kittycat Club if you let me be the president," she said.

At first I didn't know what to do. Then I said, "Okay. You can be the president, Amanda. But *I* will run the meetings."

Amanda thought for a long time. "All right," she said at last.

I nodded. "Good. Now we have a job to do. We have to deliver the fliers."

Two Best Friends

Hannie and Amanda and I worked hard. We put all the Kittycat Club fliers into mailboxes. We walked up and down our street. It took a long, long time.

"I'm sure we'll be cat-sitters very soon," I said.

Late that afternoon, Mommy and Seth came to pick up Andrew and me. It was time to go back to the little house.

"Good-bye! Good-bye!" Andrew and I called.

"Good-bye!" called Daddy and Elizabeth and Charlie and Sam and David Michael and Kristy.

I told Mommy and Seth about the Kittycat Club while we were eating dinner that night.

"I bet we'll get lots of jobs," I said. "I know all about running a business. Kristy told me about the Baby-sitters Club."

Mommy and Seth looked at each other. Seth raised his eyebrows. Mommy said, "Don't get your hopes up."

But I wasn't listening. I was daydreaming. In my daydream, everyone on Daddy's street was on vacation. And they all needed cat-sitters. The girls in the Kittycat Club were very, very busy — and very, very rich.

"Hannie! Hannie!" I called.

It was Monday. Back to school. I could see Hannie stepping into our classroom. Hannie and I are in second grade in Stoneybrook Academy. Our teacher is Ms. Colman. She's a very nice teacher.

Another person in our class is Nancy Dawes, my little-house best friend. Sometimes this is confusing because of Hannie. Hannie is my big-house best friend. And both of my best friends are in my class.

Karen Two-Two.

Hannie turned around when she heard me calling.

"Wait up!" I shouted.

Hannie waited. We walked into our room together. "Did we get any phone calls?" I asked. "Does anyone need a cat-sitter?"

"You could say 'hello' first," Hannie pointed out.

"Hello," I said. "Does anyone need a cat-sitter?"

Hannie shook her head. "Nope," she replied. "Sorry."

"Were there any calls at all?"

"Nope."

The next day, I pounced on Hannie again. "Does anyone need a cat-sitter?"

"Nope."

"Darn. The Kittycat Club is not working — yet. But it will work," I added.

"What's the Kittycat Club?" someone asked.

I turned around. Nancy Dawes was standing behind me. I guess she'd been listening to Hannie and me.

"The Kittycat Club," I began, "is our cat-sitting business."

"Who's in the club?" asked Nancy.

"Hannie and me and Amanda Delaney."

Nancy looked hurt. "How could you start a club without *me?*"

"I'm sorry," I told her. "But you can't be in this club."

"Why not?" she cried.

"Because you don't have a cat. You have to have a cat to be in the Kittycat Club. That's the rule."

"Well, I think that is very unfair. You can't have a club without your best friend."

Nancy walked away. She sat down at her desk. She put her head on her arms.

I felt awful. Two days had gone by and we had not gotten a cat-sitting call. Worse, Nancy was mad at me. I had hurt her feelings.

Boo, boo, boo.

No Jobs Yet

On Wednesday I said to Hannie, "Does anyone need a cat-sitter?"

Hannie sat down at her desk. She shook her head. "No. We haven't gotten a single call."

"Darn, darn, darn. Boo, boo, boo," I said. "I am so mad . . . I mean, I mean — Oh, well. We don't have any jobs yet. But we will soon!" Nancy Dawes had just come into our classroom. I didn't want her to think I was upset. Or that anything was wrong with the Kittycat Club.

* * *

On Thursday morning I found Hannie on the playground. We did not have to go into the school building yet. Hannie was sitting on a swing. I sat down next to her.

"Hi," said Hannie. "We didn't get any calls. No one needs a cat-sitter."

"Darn and boo," I replied. "And how did you know I was going to ask you about that?"

"Because you have asked me about it every single morning since we started the club."

"Oh."

There was an empty swing next to me. Nancy Dawes sat on it. I was in the middle, between my two best friends.

"How's the Kittycat Club?" asked Nancy.

"Great!" I answered. "We have so much fun. We'll get a job any day now. I'm sure someone will need a cat-sitter soon."

On Friday I got to school before Hannie did. I found a big red rubber ball. When

Hannie's bus arrived, Hannie ran to me. I kicked the ball to her.

She kicked it back.

"Good morning," I said. "Does anyone need a cat-sitter?"

"Nope."

I sighed.

On Saturday I could not see Hannie. There was no school and I was at the little house. So I telephoned her.

"Hi, it's me," I said.

"No one needs a cat-sitter."

"I'll call Amanda. I'll give her the bad news," I said.

"Thank you," replied Hannie. "See you on Monday."

"See you."

We hung up.

Fighting

D*ing-dong.*

"I'll get it! I'll get it!" I cried. I just love answering our bell.

I ran to the front door of the little house. I peeked out the window. Nancy was standing on our stoop. I opened the door.

"Hi, Nancy!" I said.

"Hi." Nancy sounded sort of sad.

She came inside, and we went upstairs to my bedroom. I sat on the floor.

"Karen?" began Nancy. She picked up

Goosie. She played with his paws. "I have to ask you something. *Please* can I be in the Kittycat Club? Puh-*lease?*"

I felt bad. I could see how badly Nancy wanted to be in the club. And I wanted to let her join. But I couldn't.

"Nancy, I'm really sorry. I want to — "

Nancy interrupted me. "I know, I know," she said. "Then let's start a club of our own. Okay, Karen? We'll start a new Kittycat Club. You and I will be the only people in it. I'll let you be the president. Is that a deal?"

I sighed. I *did* want to be the president. But I had already started one Kittycat Club.

"I can't do that," I said to Nancy. "I told you before. If you want to be in a Kittycat Club, you have to have a cat. And you don't have one."

"Could I borrow Goosie?" Nancy asked.

"You have to have a *real* cat. Like Boo-Boo or Pat or Priscilla. I'm sorry. That's the club rule."

"Karen, that's not fair!" cried Nancy.

Now she sounded mad. She threw Goosie onto the bed.

I ran to him. "Poor Goosie," I said.

Nancy was not listening. "Your club is stupid anyway!" she shouted. "Stupid Kittycat Club! It's not even working. You haven't gotten one single job."

"Then why do you want to be in the club?" I asked Nancy. "And anyway, we *will* get jobs. We just have not gotten any

yet." I paused, thinking. "And our club is not stupid. *You* are stupid. You are gigundo stupid!"

"Am not!"

"Are too!"

"Am not. And good-bye. I'm leaving. We are not best friends anymore."

"Forever?" I asked. I could feel tears in my eyes.

"No, just until Monday," replied Nancy. "Good-bye."

"GOOD-BYE!"

The Kittycat Club's
First Job!

On Monday, I asked Hannie if anyone needed a cat-sitter. She said no. I asked Nancy if she wanted to split a piece of gum. She said maybe. (Later she said yes.)

On Tuesday, I asked Hannie if anyone needed a cat-sitter. She said no. I asked Nancy if she wanted to come over after school. She said she would think about it. (After she thought about it, she said yes.)

On Wednesday, I asked Hannie if anyone needed a cat-sitter.

"Yup!" she replied. She was sitting at her desk, grinning.

"What?"

"I said 'yup.' Last night, a lady called. Her name is Mrs. Werner. She's going away on vacation, and she needs someone to feed Kibble. Kibble is her cat."

"And she called *us*?" For some reason, I could hardly believe it.

"Yes. She saved our flier," said Hannie.

"Well," I said. "Well . . . well now what?"

"I told her someone would come over this afternoon to talk to her about the job."

"Which one of us?" I asked. "And where does she live?"

"She lives on my street. I mean, our street. Sort of near the end. And you will have to go to her house. Amanda has a piano lesson today. I have a Brownie meeting."

I did not know what to think. "Oh, this is so exciting!" I cried. I grabbed Hannie by the arm. I jumped up and down. Then I sat at my desk.

"What's going on?" asked Nancy. She had just gotten to school. She was hanging her jacket in her cubby.

"Oh, Nancy! Nancy! We got our very first cat-sitting job! The Kittycat Club is working at last!" I cried.

"Great," said Nancy in a small voice.

"But Hannie, how am I going to get to Mrs. Werner's house today?" I asked. "And how will I feed her cat when I live way over at the little house?"

Hannie shrugged. "Why don't you see what the job is like first?"

"Okay," I replied. But I was worried. I did not know if Mommy would drive me over to Mrs. Werner's.

Mommy did drive me. I told her it was really, really, really, really important.

"I can't drive you there every time you have to feed Kibble, though," said Mommy.

"That's okay," I replied. "Maybe Hannie and Amanda will help me."

When we reached Mrs. Werner's house,

Mommy said, "Do you want me to go in with you? I know Mrs. Werner and she's very nice. So you may go alone. But if you want company, then Andrew and I will come with you."

"I better go by myself," I said.

A grown-up cat-sitter should not bring her mother with her.

I walked to Mrs. Werner's front door. I rang her bell. Soon the door opened.

"Hello?" said an old woman.

"Are you Mrs. Werner?" I asked.

"Yes, I am."

"Hi, I'm Karen Brewer. I'm your cat-sitter. I'll feed Kibble for you."

Mrs. Werner's eyes grew very wide. *"You're* the — " she started to say. Then she opened the door wider. "Come in, please."

I stepped inside. I followed Mrs. Werner into her living room.

"Please sit down," she said.

I sat in a big armchair. My feet did not touch the floor.

Mrs. Werner found our Kittycat Club flier.

"I guess my eyes aren't what they used to be," she told me. She squinted at the flier. "Doesn't this say Katie Bower and Hannah Papaddy and Amelia Delaine, ages sixteen, seventeen, and eighteen?"

"Um, no," I replied. I was getting a funny feeling in my stomach. "It — it says Karen Brewer, Hannie Papadakis, and Amanda Delaney, ages six, seven, and eight."

"Oh! Oh, my goodness." Mrs. Werner put on a pair of glasses. She stared at the flier. "Why, it certainly does. I'm so sorry, Karen. Silly me."

I wanted to cry. "Do, um, you still want me to feed Kibble?" I asked.

Mrs. Werner looked embarrassed. "Well, the truth is, honey, I was hoping to find someone a little older than you."

I nodded. "Okay. Well, if I hear about someone, I'll tell them to call you," I said. That was the grown-up thing to do.

"Thank you, Karen," replied Mrs. Werner.

"You're welcome."

I left Mrs. Werner's house. I climbed into Mommy's car.

"What happened?" she asked me.

When I told her, I started to cry.

Later, Hannie called me. "What happened?" she asked.

When I told her, I started to cry again. "We'll talk about it at our meeting on Saturday," I said. "We need a meeting. It will be very important."

Back to the Big House

I just love Fridays! On Fridays (well, on every other Friday), Andrew and I go back to the big house. Then we get to see Daddy, Elizabeth, Charlie, Sam, Kristy, David Michael, Shannon, and Boo-Boo for two whole days.

Late Friday afternoon, Mommy drove up to the big house. Andrew and I scrambled out of the car.

" 'Bye!" called Mommy. "Have fun, kids!"

" 'Bye!" we replied. "We will!"

I was feeling very happy. I wasn't worried

about old Mrs. Werner anymore. It wasn't my fault she needed new glasses. So Mrs. Werner didn't want me to feed stupid Kibble. So what? That didn't mean I couldn't be a good cat-sitter. Didn't I feed Boo-Boo and Rocky all the time?

Andrew and I ran inside. We were carrying our knapsacks. They bumped against our knees.

I threw open the front door.

"Hello! Hello, we're here!" I shouted.

Andrew didn't say anything. He set his knapsack carefully on the floor.

Suddenly, people came running. Kristy and Charlie dashed in from the kitchen. Elizabeth, Daddy, and Sam hurried out of the living room. And David Michael slid down the bannister from the second floor landing.

There were hugs all around.

David Michael said, "I caught a huge spider. It's in a jar in my room."

Andrew replied, "Is it hairy? Can I see

it?" He picked up his knapsack. He followed David Michael to his room.

"I have to inspect," I announced.

Each time I arrive at the big house, I have to make sure everything is there. I have to see that everything is in order.

I already knew all the people were there, so that was a start. I went to my room. I unpacked my knapsack. There was Moosie. There was my other Tickly. There were my

table and chairs. There were *The Witch Next Door*, my favorite book, and *Charlotte's Web*, the long book Kristy and I were reading.

I continued checking. At last I got to the kitchen. There were Daddy and Elizabeth. They were fixing dinner.

"May I help you?" I asked politely.

"You could mix these chopped vegetables together," said Daddy. He handed me a big bowl, and a plate of carrots and green peppers and cucumbers and celery. "These are for our salad."

"Okay," I replied. I began mixing. I tried not to spill anything. While I mixed, I thought about Mrs. Werner. I thought about the Kittycat Club. I thought about how we had gotten no jobs. Maybe . . . maybe no one had saved our fliers. Maybe they had thrown them away.

"Elizabeth?" I said. "You kept the Kittycat Club flier, didn't you?"

Elizabeth turned away from the stove to look at me. "Of course, sweetie. It's right there on the bulletin board. See? It's lovely."

I was glad Elizabeth thought it was lovely, but that was not the point. "Would you call the Kittycat Club if you needed a cat-sitter?" I asked.

I saw Elizabeth and Daddy look at each other. Adults always think children do not notice this. They're wrong.

"Well," Elizabeth replied after a moment, "I just can't think of how many times we would need only a cat-sitter. What about Shannon? If we went away, we would need someone to take care of Shannon, too. We'd need a *pet*-sitter."

That made sense but, well, there must be plenty of people like Mrs. Werner with just a cat or two. I would talk about it with Hannie and Amanda at our meeting the next day.

Go Home!

"We're here!" announced Hannie.

She and Amanda were standing in the doorway to my bedroom. Hannie was holding Pat, Amanda was holding Priscilla.

Boo-Boo was on my bed. When he saw Pat and Priscilla, he began to growl.

"Come in and close the door," I told my friends. "Hurry."

The girls rushed inside. They let their cats loose. The first thing Hannie said was, "I want to be the president."

Amanda didn't even look at her. "You

can't be," she replied. "I'm the president."

"Let's talk about this later," I said. "We have two problems. One is that some people think we're too young to be cat-sitters. The other is that some people don't have only cats. They have dogs, too. They need pet-sitters, not just cat-sitters."

"I want to be the president," said Hannie again.

"Did you hear what I was telling you?" I asked.

Hannie sighed. Amanda sighed. I sighed. One of the cats sighed.

"I want to go home," said Amanda. "Nothing ever happens here."

"Let's just wait till the end of the meeting," I told her. "Maybe the phone will ring. Maybe we'll get a cat-sitting job."

"Ha," said Amanda. But we waited anyway.

The phone did ring once. It was a woman who wanted to sell light bulbs and fertilizer to Daddy.

"Darn," I said.

The meeting of the Kittycat Club was almost over when two things happened. First, Hannie said for the third time, "I want to be the president."

Amanda replied, "Shut up." (Andrew and I are not supposed to say that.)

Second, Boo-Boo saw Priscilla roll over on the floor, and he decided to play. He jumped off the bed. He pounced on Priscilla. He swiped a hunk of fur out of her gorgeous fluffy tail.

"Aughh!" cried Amanda. "Oh, no! Karen, you get that dirty old cat of yours away from my beautiful one. *Now!*"

I narrowed my eyes. "I have a better idea," I said. "You take Priscilla out of here. Go home! You go, too, Hannie. I'm tired of hearing you say you want to be the president. Who cares about that? The phone isn't ringing anyway. So good-bye!"

My friends stuck their tongues out at me. Then they picked up their cats and went home.

I looked at Boo Boo. "You go away, too," I said.

Boo-Boo tore out of the room.

Help!

I stood up. I sat down again. I was very angry.

I picked up Moosie. I put him down again. Then I picked up one of my sneakers. But I didn't put it down. I threw it across the room instead.

"Karen?" called Kristy. She was down the hall in her bedroom. "What's going on in there?"

"Nothing," I replied.

But a few moments later, Kristy was standing in my doorway. I was glad to see

her. (I think maybe I threw the shoe on purpose. I needed Kristy.)

"May I come in?" she wanted to know.

I nodded.

My sister sat beside me on the bed. "Problems?" she asked. "I saw Hannie and Amanda leave. They looked sort of mad."

"They were mad," I agreed. "And *I* am mad. Very mad. Our club is not working. It just isn't. No one is calling to offer us cat-sitting jobs. Except Mrs. Werner, and she thought I was sixteen. She also thought my name was Katie Bower."

Kristy smiled.

"And Hannie and Amanda are fighting over who gets to be the president," I added. "Amanda *is* the president, but Hannie says she wants a turn. I would like a turn, too, but I don't want any more arguments.

"Plus the cats always fight," I went on. "Boo-Boo swiped some fur out of Priscilla's tail today. . . . Oh, Kristy, you have to help me. What did I do wrong?"

Kristy looked at me thoughtfully. "Karen," she said at last, "there are several kinds of clubs. One kind is just for having fun, like playing tennis or checkers. Another kind does nice things for other people, like going to nursing homes and singing songs for the patients. And some clubs are really businesses. The Baby-sitters Club is like that. If you run a business, you have to know what you're doing. It isn't easy."

I looked down at Moosie. I sat him in my lap.

"I guess I made some mistakes with the Kittycat Club," I said.

"A few, maybe," agreed Kristy. "But everyone makes mistakes."

I sighed. "What were mine?"

"Do you really want to know?"

"I really do."

"Okay. Well, first of all, to run a good business, you have to provide a service — you know, say you'll do something that people need. Like baby-sit."

"Or cat-sit?"

"We-ell," said Kristy slowly. "You need to do something a *lot* of people need. Not too many people need just cat-sitters."

I nodded. I remembered what Elizabeth had said. "But a lot of people need baby-sitters?" I asked Kristy.

"Plenty," she replied. "The other thing is that people should really want to hire the workers who are in the business. You and Hannie and Amanda are terrific. But Mrs. Werner thought you were too young. I think other people might feel that way, too."

"Kristy, did you know these things all along?" I asked.

Kristy looked embarrassed. "Yes," she replied.

"Well, why didn't you tell me before we started the club?"

"Because I wanted to let you find out for yourself. I thought it would mean more to you. Anyway, what would you have done if I'd said, 'Karen, you're too young to start the Kittycat Club'?"

"I would have started it anyway."

"I know," said Kristy.

I grinned at her. "I better go," I said. "I have to make some phone calls."

No More Kittycat Club

I called Hannie and Amanda. I asked them to come back to my house. I asked them to leave Pat and Priscilla at home.

That was another thing, I thought, as I waited for my friends. Amanda asked why we brought our cats to the meetings. Why *did* we? We ran a cat-sitting service. Who cared if our cats came to the meetings? And why did I say Nancy could not be in the club? Why did she have to have a cat to be in it? Was this a cat club or a sitting business? I guess I had not decided.

I heard footsteps in the hall. Soon Hannie was sitting on the floor in my room. Then Amanda was next to her. They looked very serious.

I guess I looked serious, too. I felt serious.

"I — I have some things to say," I began. I slid off the bed and sat on the floor with my friends. "I don't think the Kittycat Club is a very good idea. It isn't going to work."

"Why not?" asked Hannie.

I told her and Amanda what Kristy had said. I told them what I had thought about — that I had never decided what the club was.

"I have something else to say," I added.

"What?" asked Amanda.

"I — I'm sorry."

There. I had said it. It isn't easy to say you're sorry.

"Sorry about what?" asked Hannie.

About what? Didn't she know? "I'm sorry I got mad at you guys. And I'm sorry I made you bring your cats to the meetings. I hope Priscilla's tail will be okay," I added.

"I guess it will be," replied Amanda. "It

looks a little bare. But it isn't bleeding or anything. Boy, if it were bleeding — "

"But it isn't," I said quickly. "And now, we have one more thing to do."

"We do?" said Hannie.

I nodded. "Yes. We have to end the club."

"Can't we just leave your room?" asked Amanda. "And go home?"

Honestly. Amanda has no imagination.

"I think we should give back our titles," I said. "We should have a ceremony. Amanda, you should become the un-president, I should become the un-vice-president, and Hannie should become the un-secretary."

"But how?" asked Amanda.

"Let's think."

We thought.

"I know!" cried Hannie. She whispered in my ear.

"Great idea," I said.

I looked in my dress-up box. I found a silver wand.

"This is magic," I told my friends, holding

up the wand. "It has secret powers. Now, Amanda, you stand up. Since you're the president, you'll make me the un-vice-president. Then you'll make Hannie the un-secretary. You'll say, um, 'Secret powers, do your tricks.' "

"But what about me? Who will make me the un-president?" asked Amanda.

"Hmm." I thought about that. Then I said, "You can do it. You're the president.

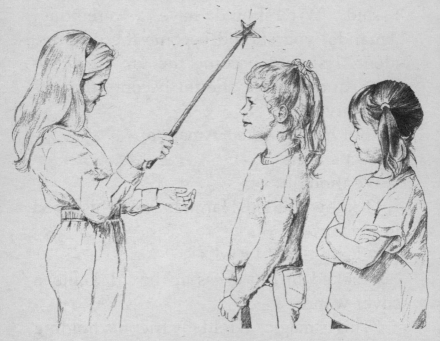

You can make yourself the un-president."

"Okay," said Amanda. She touched me, then Hannie, then herself with the silver wand.

We were un-club members.

The Kittycat Club was over.

Sad, Glad

Hannie and Amanda left for the second time that day. I sat in my room. I was alone except for Moosie, Tickly, my nineteen stuffed animals, and my seven dolls.

"Blah, blah, blah. Blechh, blechh, blechh," I said grumpily.

I looked at myself in the mirror. I pulled the corners of my mouth down. I tried to make tears come out of my eyes. Instead, I found that if I rubbed the top of my nose, I could make myself sneeze.

"Achoo! Achoo!"

"Karen? Are you getting a cold?" called Kristy.

"No." I stopped rubbing my nose. If I kept on sneezing, someone might make me take medicine.

I looked in the mirror again. I tried to think of a really sad song. It was hard. Most of the sad ones I know are for big people. One is about feelings. It goes, *"Feelings. Woe-woe-woe feelings."* The other one has better words. It goes, *"Memories, like the corners of my eyes. Misty watercolor memories of the way we were."* (Or something like that.)

"Oh, that is *so sad*," I told Moosie. "I'm not sure what it means, but it does seem awfully sad. It's all about losing something. Just like that other song. The one that goes, *'Does your chewing gum lose its flavor on the bedpost overnight?'* "

I was nearly in tears. Imagine losing the flavor of your chewing gum.

"Oh, Moosie, Moosie, Moosie," I said.

I sat on my bed and held Moosie in my arms. *"Hush-a-bye, baby,"* I sang to him, *"on the treetop! When the wind blows the cradle will rock; When the bough breaks the cradle will fall; Down will come baby, bough, cradle, and all.''* I set Moosie on the bed. "Sorry, Moosie, that was an awful song, a sad song. Think about it. The cradle *falls*, with the baby in it."

I turned Moosie upside down so that his smile was going in the wrong direction. "There," I said, "you look awfully sad. Just like I feel."

Sitting next to Moosie was my doll, Amelia Jane. I turned her upside down, too. Then my stuffed giraffe, my stuffed monkey, Tessie the talking doll, and a few more.

I was about halfway finished when I stopped to see how my bed looked.

It looked funny. I began to laugh. Half of my dolls and animals were upside down and pouting. The other half were rightside up and smiling.

I couldn't stop laughing. This was one of the silliest things I'd ever done. Having fun

sure was a lot better than having a club. . . .
Wait a sec. Hadn't Kristy said that some
clubs *were* for fun? For playing tennis or
something?

I began to smile. I turned the upside-
down animals rightside up.

Fun . . .

Did I dare to start another club? Would
another club work? I didn't know. But I
decided that it was worth finding out about.

Karen and Nancy

Ialmost ran over to Hannie's house. I was going to say, "I have a great idea for another club. Want to help me start it?"

But I didn't go. I was sure Hannie was tired of my clubs. Besides, there was someone else who would want to help me start a new club. And it was time to call that person.

I went into our kitchen. Sam was there. He was eating a sandwich. I didn't want to make the phone call in front of Sam.

I went into the family room. David Michael and Andrew were there. They were watching a scary movie on TV. I didn't want to make the call in front of David Michael and Andrew, either.

"Elizabeth!" I called.

"I'm in the living room," she answered.

"Elizabeth," I said, when I had found her, "may I please use the phone in your bedroom? I need to make a private call."

Elizabeth said I could use the phone.

I ran upstairs to Daddy and Elizabeth's room. I closed the door. Then I lay across the bed and picked up the phone. I dialed Nancy's number.

Nancy answered herself. This is what she said: "Hello, this is Nancy Dawes speaking. Who is this, please?" Her parents tell her to do that, but she does not always remember.

I giggled. "This is Karen Brewer speaking. Is this *really* Nancy Dawes?"

Nancy laughed. "It's the one and only famous Nancy Dawes."

"Look, Nancy — " I began.

"Look at what? I don't see anything."

"Nancy, stop. I have to say some things, and they're really important."

"Okay." Nancy stopped laughing.

"Well, first of all, I'm — " (here we go again) " — I'm sorry. I'm really sorry I wouldn't let you be in the Kittycat Club. I wasn't trying to be mean."

"But why did you keep telling me I had to have a cat? I could cat-sit without a cat."

"I know. I just wasn't thinking, I guess."

"Does this mean I can be in the club?" asked Nancy. She sounded very excited.

"I wish it did, but the Kittycat Club is over."

"It's over?"

"Yes." I told Nancy what had happened.

"Boo," she said.

"But wait. Then I got this other idea," I went on. "See, Kristy told me there are all kinds of clubs. And she said some clubs are just for fun. And I still want to have a club. But I want a club that anyone can join. And I want a club with no rules and no presidents."

"That sounds good," said Nancy.

"Would you help me start a club like that?" I asked. "We wouldn't be in charge or anything. We would just *start* the club. And then be in it."

"Sure I'll help!" cried Nancy.

"What kind of club will it be?" I asked.

"You mean our fun club?"

"That's it!" I exclaimed. "That's what it will be! The Fun Club!"

"I like that," said Nancy.

"And we can hold meetings at my houses. The big house or the little house. Wherever I am."

"And anyone can come," added Nancy. "Whenever they want."

"And we'll play and have fun. That's *all* we'll do."

"We'll tell everyone at school about it!" said Nancy.

"Right," I replied. "Boy, how are we ever going to wait until Monday?"

The Fun Club

"Do you think anyone will come? Do you think anyone will come?"

"*Karen,*" replied my mother. I had asked her this question a lot of times. She was getting tired of hearing it. "Yes. I think your friends will come."

It was Tuesday. The day before, Nancy and I had told practically everyone in school about the Fun Club. Now I was waiting to see if anyone would come. It was three-thirty. The Fun Club was supposed to start at four.

"What's your Fun Club going to do?" asked Andrew.

He stood next to me at the front door of the little house. We were watching to see if anyone would come early.

"Play," I told him.

"Can I play, too?" he asked.

I almost said, "No. You're too little." Then I remembered the rules. Anyone can come to the Fun Club. "Sure," I said. "If you want."

"Goody," replied Andrew.

At a quarter to four, the doorbell rang. There was Nancy. "I'm here!" she announced.

Five minutes later, the bell rang again. There were Hannie and Amanda. "We're here!" they said.

The doorbell rang again and again. Four more girls from school came: Heather, Nina, Kim, and Vicky.

I counted the people in the Fun Club.

"Nine!" I exclaimed. "Eight girls plus Andrew."

"Yuck!" said Andrew. "Eight girls. Forget it. I don't want to be in this club." He ran to his room.

"Well, the rest of us are going to have fun," I said. "Right?"

"Right!"

"What do you want to do first?" I asked.

"Put on a play," said Nancy.

So we went into the rec room, where we would have plenty of space. We performed "Cinderella." We invited Andrew to come watch, but he stayed in his room. Mommy watched by herself.

Then Mommy said it would be okay to make a mess in the kitchen, so we got out newspaper and flour and water, and I found some balloons. We made heads for puppets. We decided that at the next club meeting, we could paint the heads. And at the *next* meeting, we could make bodies. My puppet was going to be a present for Andrew.

The girls in the Fun Club cleaned up the kitchen. Then we went back to the rec room. We lay on the floor on our stomachs.

"Let's tell jokes," said Vicky.

"I know a good one," I said. "What did Tarzan say when he saw the elephants coming?"

"What?" asked Heather.

"He said, 'Here come the elephants.'" (My friends groaned.) "But," I went on, "what did he say when he saw them coming wearing sunglasses?"

"What?" asked Heather again.

"Nothing. He didn't recognize them!"

We were all giggling. We told some more jokes. When we ran out of jokes, we sang songs. And then my friends' parents began to arrive. The first meeting of the Fun Club was over.

"Good-bye! Good-bye!" I called as everyone left. At last, only Nancy and I were standing at the front door.

"I think the Fun Club will work," I said. "I really do. I'll call Kristy and tell her."

Nancy smiled. "Good-bye, Kittycat Club," she said.

And I replied, "Hello, Fun Club!"

About the Author

ANN M. MARTIN lives in New York City and loves animals. Her cat, Mouse, knows how to take the phone off the hook.

Other books by Ann M. Martin that you might enjoy are *Stage Fright*, *Me and Katie (the Pest)*, and the books in *The Baby-sitters Club* series.

Ann likes ice cream, the beach, and *I Love Lucy*. And she has her own little sister, whose name is Jane.

Little Sister

by Ann M. Martin
author of The Baby-sitters Club®

More Titles... ➡